For Carole

WHAT IF?

Verse and pictures by
ROBERT PIERCE

ISBN: 1-40372-350-8
15179/0606 What If

Printed in the U.S.A.
06 07 08 09 LBM 10 9 8 7 6 5 4 3 2 1

WHAT IF an elephant
Climbed your stairs?

What if your closet
Was full of bears?

What if a kangaroo
Came to cook?

And a tiger read you
A story book?

What if a seal
And a tall giraffe
Did magic tricks
To make you laugh?

If all this happened,
What would you do?
The answer is easy—

START A ZOO!

What if an ostrich,
All in a dither,

Danced to the tune
Of a zebra's zither?

What if some yaks
And a unicorn
Played drums and sax
And a big bass horn?

What could you do
With the noise they made?
What do you think?

HAVE A PARADE!

AT-A-
AT TAT HONK TWING
TWANG RAZZAZZA
MAZZAZZ

WHAT IF birthdays
Came twice a week?

And behind your house
Was a lemonade creek?

What if rocks
Were made of cheese?

And baseballs grew
On baseball trees?

What if cookies fell
And hit your nose?

And ice cream oozed
From the garden hose?

What if your friends
Were jolly and hearty?
What would you do?

HAVE A PARTY!

WHAT IF a green
And purple snake—

Gobbled up all
Of the birthday cake?

What if your bathtub
Was full of frogs?

What if it <u>really</u> rained
Cats and dogs?

What if a crocodile
Big as an ox—

Hid in the hallway
And ate your socks?

Or a lion was having
A masquerade ball—
    What would you do?

INVITE THEM ALL!